Life in Unusual Places

Julia Wall

Life in Unusual Places

Text: Julia Wall
Editor: Ben Haskin
Design: Jennifer Warwick
Series design: James Lowe
Photo researcher: Corrina Tauschke
Production controllers: Renee Cusmano and Lisa Porter

Acknowledgements
The author and publisher would like to acknowledge permission to reproduce material from the following sources:
Alamy/Visual&Written SL: p. 8; Corbis/Construction Photography: p. 11; Corbis/George Steinmetz: p. 17; Corbis/Goebel/zefa: p. 12; Corbis/Steve Kaufman: p. 6; Getty Images: pp. 7, 19, 20, back cover; iStockphoto: p. 4; Lonely Planet Image/Johnny Haglund: p. 16; Photolibrary/Ariadne Van Zandbergen: pp. 1, 14, cover; Photolibrary/Gavin Hellier: p. 15; Photolibrary/Jon Arnold Images: pp. 3, 18; Photolibrary/NASA/Science Photo Library: p. 21; Photolibrary/Robin Laurance: p. 5; Photolibrary/Science Photo Library: p. 13; REUTERS/Greg Locke: p. 10; REX FEATURES/AUSTRAL: pp. 9, 23; Tom Chudleigh/Free Spirit Spheres: p. 22.

Fast Forward Independent Texts
Level 19

ISBN 978 0 17 017928 7
ISBN 978 0 17 017898 3 (set)

Cengage Learning Australia
Level 7, 80 Dorcas Street
South Melbourne, Victoria Australia 3205
Phone: 1300 790 853

Cengage Learning New Zealand
Unit 4B Rosedale Office Park
331 Rosedale Road, Albany, North Shore NZ 0632
Phone: 0800 449 725

For learning solutions, visit **cengage.com.au**

Printed in Australia by Ligare Pty Ltd
2 3 4 5 6 7 8 22 21 20 19 18

Life in Unusual Places

Julia Wall

Contents

Where People Live

Everyone in the world
needs a place to live.
Most people live in houses in cities or towns.

Some people live in very unusual places
that are **remote** or difficult to live in.
Sometimes people go to live in an unusual place
to work there.
Sometimes people live their whole lives
in an unusual place.

People live in many different unusual places.

CHAPTER 2

Living at Sea

Submarines

Some people spend time living under the sea.
People who work on **submarines**
don't spend all their time under the water.
But when a submarine dives,
they must be ready for life
under the sea.

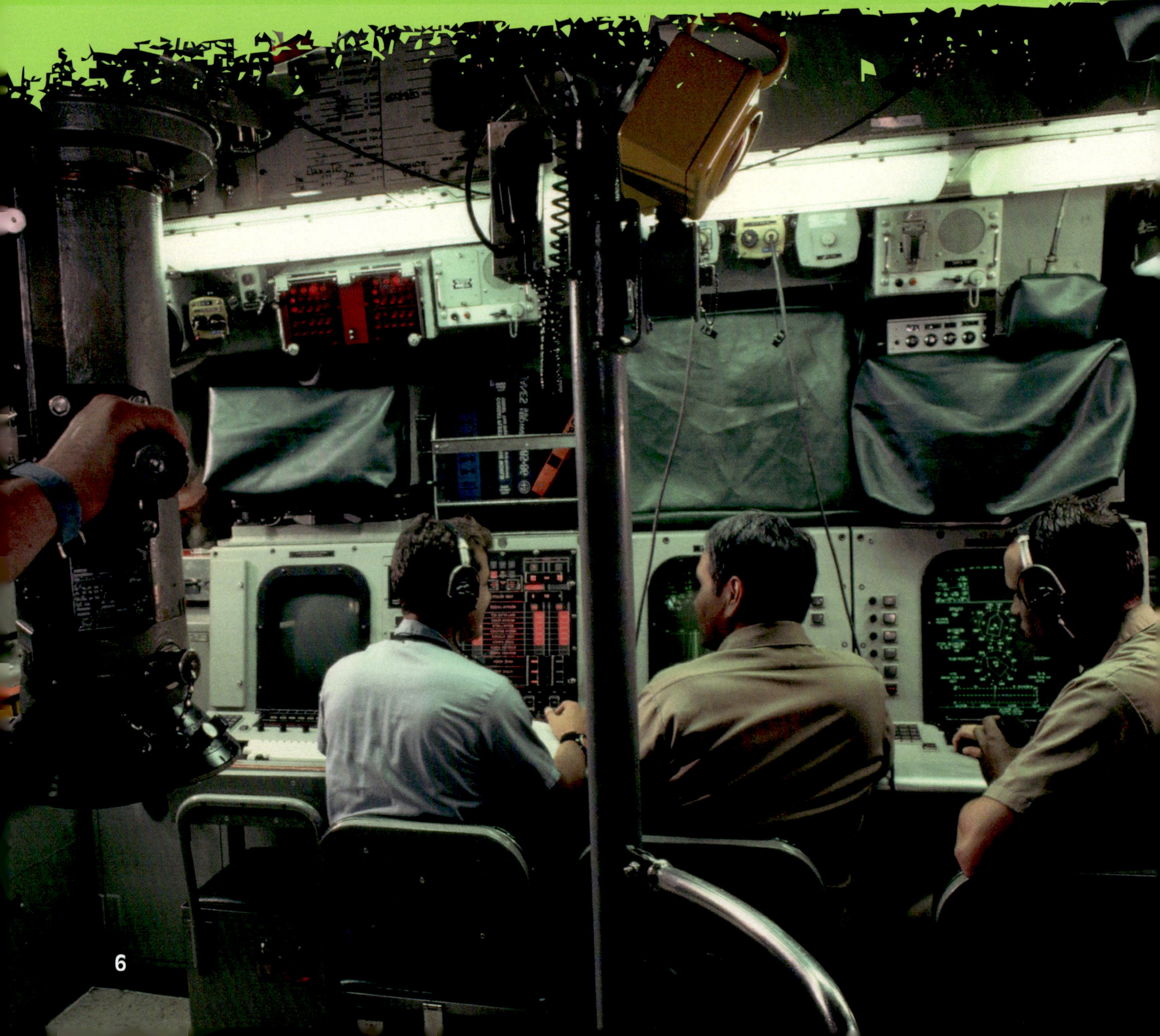

Sailors on a submarine live in crowded ***conditions****.*
There is not much privacy.

Submarines can travel on the surface of the water
or under the water.
When a submarine **submerges**,
the sailors must stay inside the submarine.
Everything they need
must be carried in the submarine,
including air, drinking water and food.

Marine Laboratories

There is only one **marine laboratory** in the world,
and it is called Aquarius.
It is 19 metres underwater,
about six kilometres off the coast of Florida in the USA.
Scientists sometimes live on Aquarius
for a short time.

The scientists carry out marine research
and stay on Aquarius
until their **mission** is finished.
Missions usually last about ten days.

Being underwater is a lot like being in space,
so astronauts also stay on Aquarius
as part of their training
for space travel.

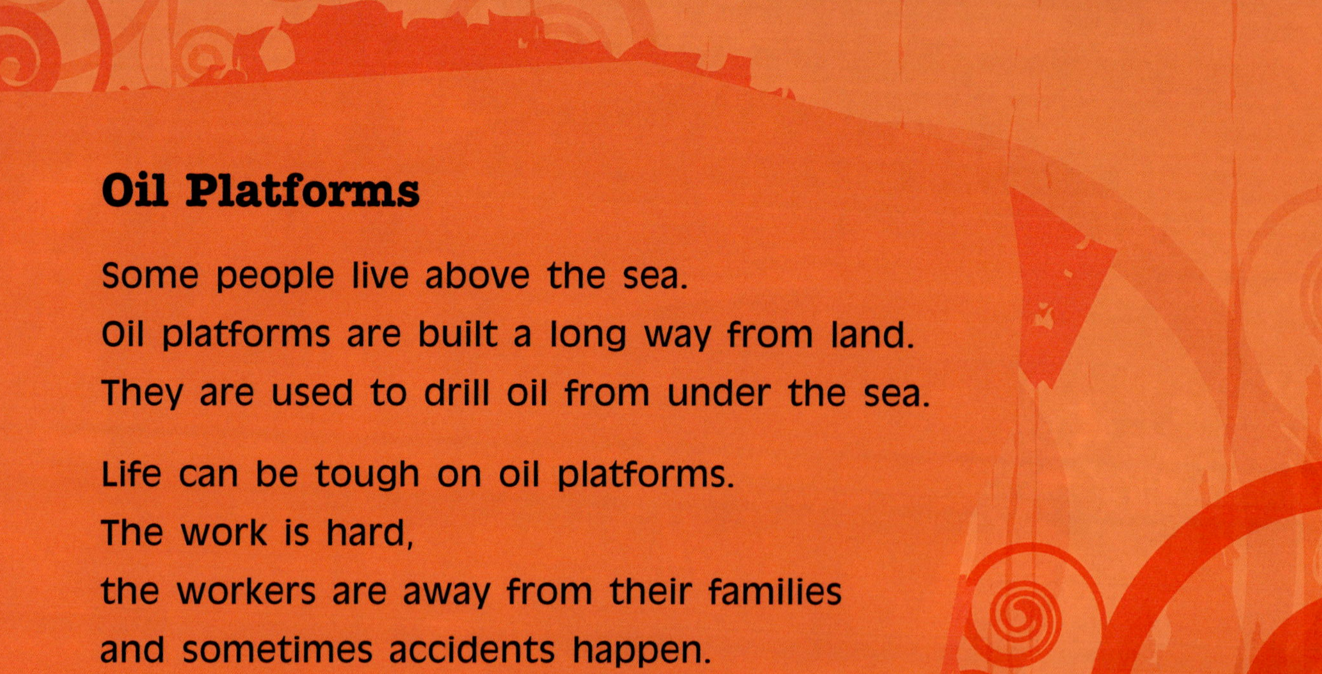

Oil Platforms

Some people live above the sea.
Oil platforms are built a long way from land.
They are used to drill oil from under the sea.

Life can be tough on oil platforms.
The work is hard,
the workers are away from their families
and sometimes accidents happen.

The Hibernia Platform is the largest oil platform in the world.

flying to an oil platform

Because they are in the middle of the ocean,
oil platforms are hard to get to.
People who work on oil platforms
have to fly to the platform by helicopter.
They usually stay for two weeks at a time,
then have two weeks at home.

Living on the Land

Antarctica

Antarctica is the coldest **continent** on Earth.
For this reason,
scientists are interested in studying
the Antarctic environment,
including the animals and plants
that live there.

Getting to Antarctica is not easy.
It is far away and weather conditions
can make travel hard.
Most people go to Antarctica in the summer
and leave before winter sets in.

travelling by ship to Antarctica

But there are a few people who stay in Antarctica all year. Some countries have set up bases there. Scientists live on the bases with **support people** who keep the bases running.

The buildings are made to handle the extreme weather.

The Amundsen–Scott South Pole Station is run by the USA.

Deserts

Living in very hot conditions can be just as difficult as living in the extreme cold.

Deserts make up one-third of Earth's land area. They get very little rain.

In a desert,
it is usually very hot during the day
and very cold at night.
People who live in deserts
must take care to stay cool during the day.

Some deserts have sandstorms, which can make it hard to breathe.

People who live in sandy deserts cover their faces in case a sandstorm hits.

Tree Houses

There is a group of people in West Papua, Indonesia, who make their homes in trees. They usually build their tree houses on poles, up to 25 metres above the ground.

There are **swampy** forests in the area that they live in. Living in a tree house helps the people to stay dry, and keeps them safe from animals.

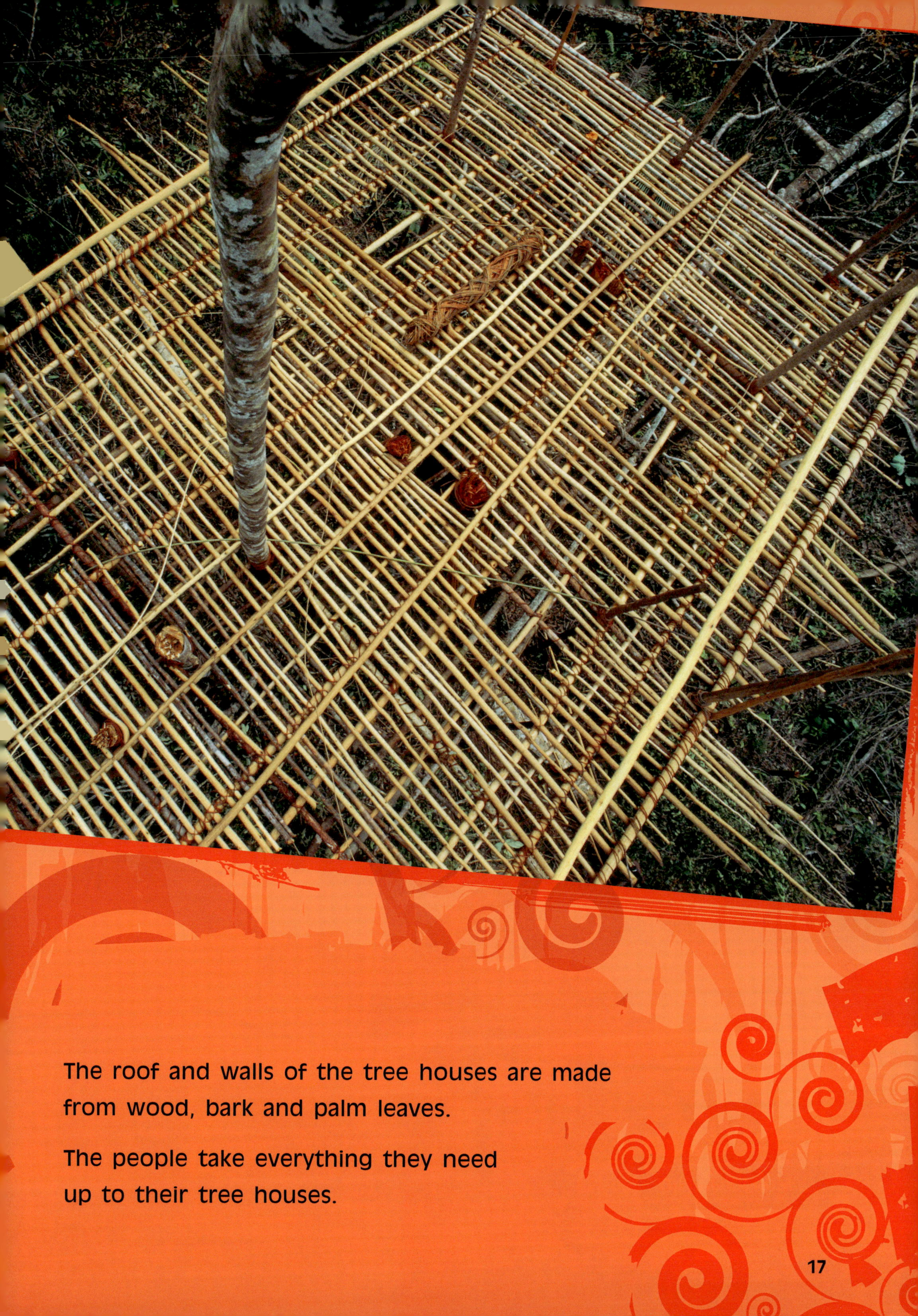

The roof and walls of the tree houses are made from wood, bark and palm leaves.

The people take everything they need up to their tree houses.

Mountains

Mongolia is the highest country on Earth, so Mongolians are used to living in high places.

a Mongolian yurt

Mount Everest, in Nepal, is the highest mountain in the world.
Climbing it is very difficult.

People who try to climb it must live on the mountain for weeks.
The higher they go, the harder it is to breathe.
They face very cold and windy weather.

The conditions on Mount Everest are dangerous, and many people who have tried to climb it have died there.

Living in Space

Astronauts can live on the International Space Station.

Life on a space station is very different
from life on Earth.
There is not much room to move.

In space, things float around
because there is less **gravity** there.
Astronauts tie their sleeping bags to the wall,
so that they don't float around
while they are asleep.

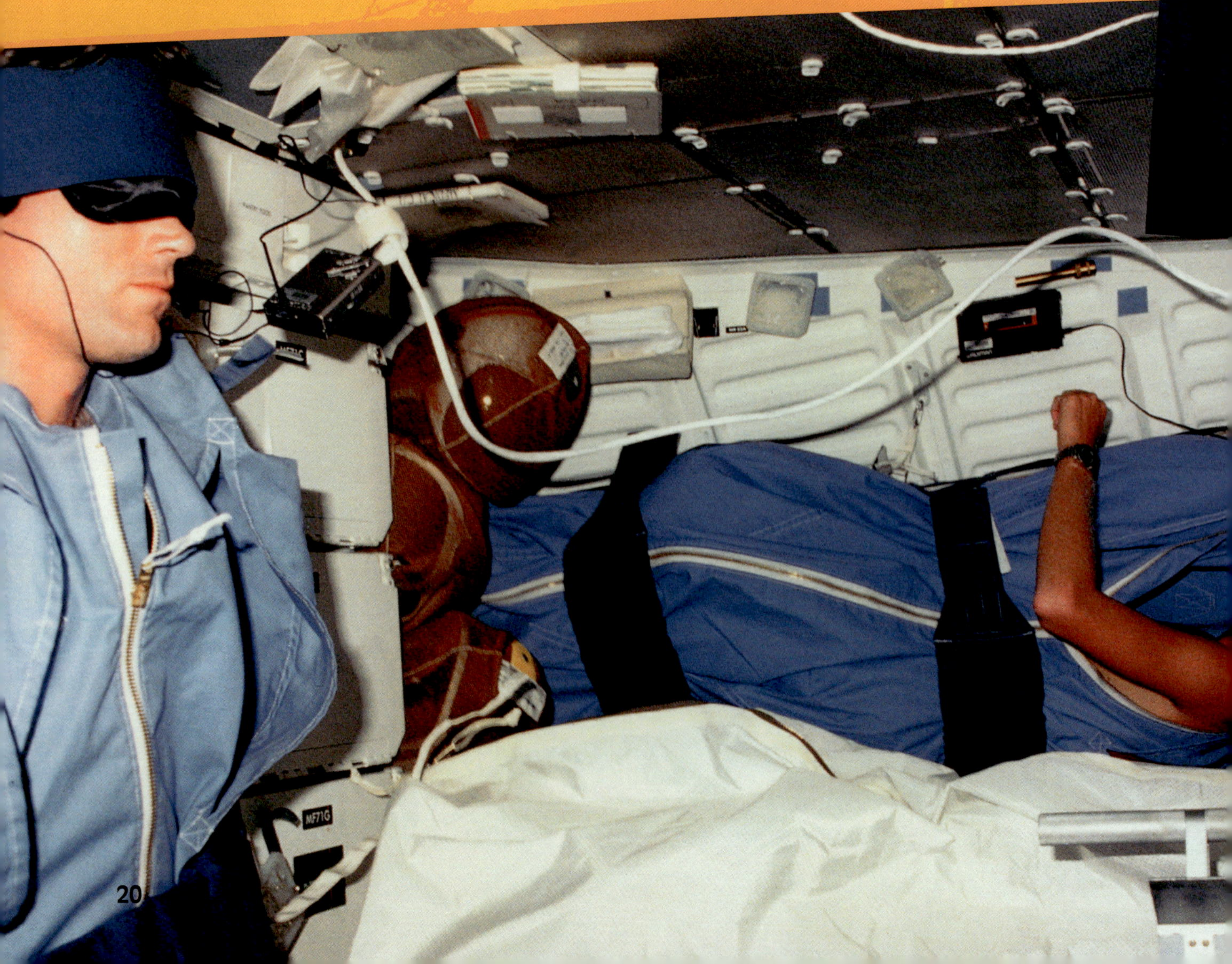

Up in space,
astronauts have to hold on
to their food
or it will float away!

CHAPTER 5

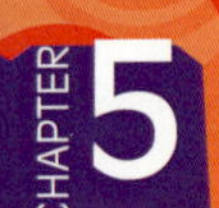

Weird and Wonderful Places

People live in all sorts of weird and wonderful places around the world.

Sometimes people live in unusual buildings, or they may not live in a building at all.

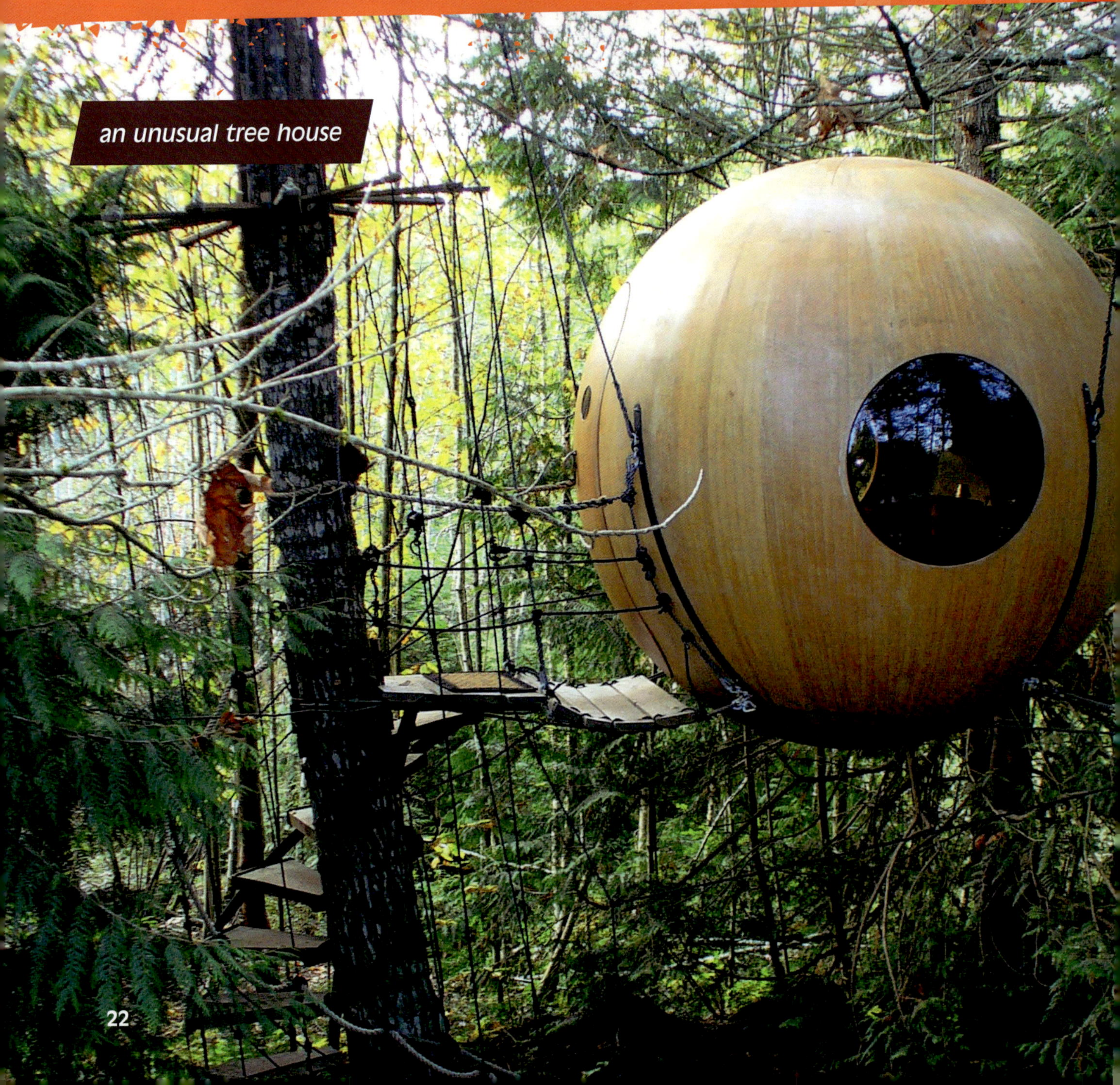

an unusual tree house

People live in unusual places because they work there, for cultural reasons or because they like living in an interesting place.

This wooden building in far north-west Russia is nearly 44 metres tall.

Glossary

conditions	things that affect people, such as the weather
continent	a large block of land surrounded by sea
gravity	the force that makes things fall to Earth
marine laboratory	a place for research under the sea
mission	a special task that needs to be done
remote	far away
submarines	underwater boats
submerges	goes under water
support people	people such as cleaners, cooks and those who make repairs
swampy	ground that is always muddy

Index